OXFORD
UNIVERSITY PRESS

Great Clarendon Street, Oxford OX2 6DP

Oxford University Press is a department of the University of Oxford.
It furthers the University's objective of excellence in research, scholarship,
and education by publishing worldwide in

Oxford New York

Athens Auckland Bangkok Bogotá Buenos Aires
Cape Town Chennai Dar es Salaam Delhi Florence Hong Kong Istanbul
Karachi Kolkata Kuala Lumpur Madrid Melbourne Mexico City Mumbai
Nairobi Paris São Paulo Shanghai Singapore Taipei Tokyo Toronto Warsaw

with associated companies in Berlin Ibadan

Oxford is a registered trade mark of Oxford University Press
in the UK and in certain other countries

British Library Cataloguing in Publication Data available

ISBN 0 19 272503 3

3 5 7 9 10 8 6 4 2

Printed in Malaysia

ARTHUR CONAN DOYLE'S
THE HOUND OF THE BASKERVILLES

Adapted and Illustrated by Chris Mould

OXFORD
UNIVERSITY PRESS

THE CURSE

Mr Sherlock Holmes and I were seated at breakfast. A great mystery, which only Holmes could unravel, was headed for our door.

'In the seventeenth century, Baskerville Hall was held by Sir Hugo Baskerville. He loved a local maiden but when she rejected him, he stole away with her on his horse one night.

The arrival of Dr Mortimer was no surprise to us; he had called earlier and we were expecting him.

'How may we help you?' enquired Holmes.

'I have a manuscript which was given to me by Sir Charles Baskerville of Devonshire, who has recently died. It is about a legend that runs in the family. May I read it to you?'

'She was locked up in the hall, but managed to escape. Sir Hugo went across the moonlit moor after her. His men followed them, and eventually found their bodies. A great black hound with blazing eyes and dripping jaws stood over them.

'That is the legend of the Baskervilles. Now Sir Charles Baskerville is dead. His heart was weak, and he was found outside at night, without a mark on him. But when I examined the ground nearby I saw the footprints of a large hound.'

'A hound, with burning eyes and a mouth of fire, is often seen on the moor. Sir Henry Baskerville, the heir, arrives from America today. I fear for his safety.'

The next morning Dr Mortimer returned with Sir Henry, who gave Holmes a letter he had received. It warned him to stay away from the moor.

'And there's something else strange,' said Sir Henry. 'I left my boots for cleaning last night. This morning one was missing.'

Despite hearing the legend of the hound, Sir Henry was adamant that he would go to his family home. We agreed to meet later at his hotel.

But when Sir Henry and Dr Mortimer left, Holmes and I followed them at a safe distance, in the hope that we might learn something.

Suddenly we noticed a cab. Inside it, a bearded man was watching them closely. When he saw us, the cab was off. Holmes tried to follow, but to no avail.

'At least I have the cab number,' said Holmes.

Baskerville Hall

When we all met again, Holmes asked Sir [H] his intentions.

'I shall go to Baskerville Hall,' he replied.

'Very well,' said Holmes. 'But you must not [ ] alone. Dr Watson will accompany you.'

Holmes had by now caught up with the cab driver—who told him that the name given by his bearded passenger was Sherlock Holmes!

Our journey to Dartmoor was swift and pleasant. We left the train and rode across the moor in a carriage. There we met an armed policeman on a horse.

'What is this?' cried Dr Mortimer.

'A convict has escaped from the prison,' said our driver. 'Selden, the Notting Hill murderer.'

The road ahead grew bleaker and wilder. Huge trees, twisted by years of storms, surrounded us. Then two turrets rose up above. 'Baskerville Hall, sir,' said our driver.

Soon we were in front of the house. A tall figure appeared from the porch.

Another figure appeared. The two were Mr and Mrs Barrymore, the butler and housekeeper.

'Welcome to Baskerville Hall, Sir Henry,' they said.

Barrymore was bearded like the spy in the cab, and that night I was awoken by the sound of a woman crying. What secrets did this gloomy place hold?

Sir Henry had also heard the crying, but when we consulted Barrymore he insisted that it wasn't his wife. Yet her eyes looked red and swollen. I decided to report this to Holmes.

'We were sorry about Sir Charles,' continued Stapleton. And he told me again of the fiendish dog that haunted Dartmoor. Just then a low moan swept across the moor. 'Hear that? Some say it is the cry of the hound.'

And then, suddenly, he was off, chasing a butterfly.

After breakfast I walked out onto the moor. A man called out to me, introducing himself: 'I'm Stapleton, of Merripit House,' he said. 'I'm a naturalist.'

I heard the sound of footsteps and turned to greet a handsome woman, Miss Stapleton, the sister of my new acquaintance.

'Go back to London!' she cried. 'Keep away from here!'

She had taken me to be Sir Henry, but I could not understand her warning.

Dear Holmes

Dear Holmes,

Let me give you some facts about this strange place. We have seen nothing of the escaped prisoner. He could hide here, but he would have n food. My guess is that he has moved on.

Mr Barrymore also intrigues me. I was woken again in the night, by footsteps. It was Barrymore. He carried a candle and passed down the corridor into an empty room.

There appears to be a mutual attraction between Sir Henry and Miss Stapleton. One would imagine that Stapleton would welcome this, but he seems to disapprove.

Mrs Barrymore interests me. I told you of her sobbing in the night. I am convinced she is hiding some secret sorrow.

I watched him further. He crouched at the window and held up the candle as he stared across the moor. After some time he put out the light. There is some secret business going on here. I shall write again when there is more to tell you.

Watson

Baskerville Hall
15th October

Dear Holmes,

Today I followed Sir Henry as he walked across the moor, where he met Miss Stapleton.

I soon realized that I was not the only onlooker. Stapleton's butterfly net caught my eye, and I saw there was some quarrel between the three. What this was about I could not tell.

I caught up with Sir Henry as he walked back to the Hall. He explained that he had asked Miss Stapleton to marry him. Stapleton had heard, and lost his temper. But in the afternoon, Stapleton came to apologize.

'I'm sorry, but my sister is all I have here. I did not mean to be rude.'

And we were invited to the Stapleton's home on Friday.

The Barrymore mystery is solved. Sir Henry and I found Barrymore at the window again. He and Mrs Barrymore explained that Selden is Mrs Barrymore's brother. The candle signals that there is food for him.

'He has the reputation of an evil man, but to me he will always be my little brother,' she told me, crying.

Sir Henry and I went out in search of Selden. We caught a glimpse of him running away, but we also saw a taller, dark figure in the distance. It is all very strange.

Watson

We decided it was better to let Selden escape, and in his gratitude Barrymore came forward with some useful information. 'It's something I found long after Sir Charles died.'

'The night Sir Charles died,' continued Barrymore, 'he was meeting a woman. My wife found part of a letter in the fire. It said, "Please burn this letter and be at the gate by ten o'clock." It was signed L. L.'

If I could discover the identity of L. L. we would be somewhat nearer a solution.

Later I walked out again upon the moor. Dr Mortimer came by in his carriage and gave me a lift back to the Hall. He told me of a woman in Coombe Tracey called Laura Lyons – L. L. Later, I talked with Barrymore. He too knew of the tall man on the moor. Selden had spoken to him, but had not known his identity. When would we solve this tangled web of mysteries?

The following day I had to establish two important facts about Sir Charles's death. Had Laura Lyons written to him and arranged to see him? And who was this man lurking on the moor?

After that, I searched every corner of the moor. I discovered a circle of stone huts; one was in good repair. I went inside. The ashes of a recent fire still smouldered.

There was nobody there, but suddenly I heard footsteps. I drew my pistol and waited.

When I reached Coombe Tracey, Miss Lyons was at work in her office. She agreed that she had been going to meet Sir Charles to ask him for financial help. But in the end she did not keep her appointment, because she received help from someone else.

I couldn't help feeling that she was keeping something back from me.

'It's a lovely evening, Watson.'

'Holmes!' I cried; and there he was, with a wry smile, and his pipe smoking in his mouth.

I was never so glad to see anyone as I was to see Holmes just then. But why was he out here?

'My dear fellow, I have been secretly following the investigation from a different point of view. My own findings tell me that a close intimacy exists between Stapleton and Miss Lyons. And Miss Stapleton is really his wife, not his sister.'

Suddenly Stapleton's objections to Sir Henry became clear. But why this deception? We were now very suspicious of Stapleton.

'Stapleton thought that his wife would be more useful if people thought she was single. And it was Stapleton in the cab in London,' continued Holmes. 'So, we are closing in on him.'

Suddenly an awful scream filled the air, followed by the dreadful sound which I know to be the hound. We searched high and low and eventually found a body—it was wearing Sir Henry's red tweed coat.

But the body was not Sir Henry. Holmes recognized it as the convict. I remembered that Sir Henry gave some of his old clothes to Barrymore, who must have passed them on.

Stapleton soon appeared on the scene. He seemed disappointed not to see Sir Henry.

Back at the Hall, Sir Henry was pleased to see Holmes. We broke the news of Selden's death to Mrs Barrymore, who wept bitterly.

Later, Holmes looked at the portraits in the Hall. He was very interested in the wicked Sir Hugo.

That night he led me back and held a candle up. 'Look carefully,' he said.

Suddenly, I saw Stapleton's face. Was Stapleton really a Baskerville, and hoping to inherit the Hall?

The next morning Holmes and I told Sir Henry that we were going to London.

'You will have to go on your own to dinner at the Stapletons' tonight,' said Holmes. 'Make sure that you walk home.'

We then went to see Laura Lyons. Holmes told her that Stapleton's supposed sister was his wife, and she decided to reveal all. 'Stapleton dictated the letter requesting the meeting,' she said. 'And then told me not to go.' This ensured Sir Charles was out alone that night

Holmes and I did not return to London. Instead, we made our way to Merripit House.

We stopped behind some rocks, a hundred yards from the house. A dense fog was closing in.

We fired our pistols and the beast fell dead. Sir Henry was shocked, but not hurt. Phosphorus covered the hound's open mouth. 'Trickery,' said Holmes.

Eventually Sir Henry left the house for the walk home. The fog closed in. Then, suddenly, we saw a huge hound spring out of the mist. Fire burst from its mouth, and its eyes glowed.

'He kept the beast on the moor, at a tin mine surrounded by a bog,' she replied.

But Stapleton could not have found his way to it that night. The next day, all we could find in the bog was Sir Henry's missing boot. Stapleton had used it to give his scent to the hound.

Stapleton had fled from Merripit House, but we found his wife in an upstairs room.

'Where has he gone?' asked Holmes.

We were back in Baker Street. Dartmoor was a distant memory, but there was still much that was not clear to me, and Holmes explained.

'Stapleton was a long-lost Baskerville. He changed his identity when he discovered that only two lives lay between him and a large estate. Sir Charles and Sir Henry. He heard of the legend and bought a huge dog which he kept on the moor. He lured Sir Charles out at night and set the dog at him, with phosphorus blazing like fire from its jaws. This finished Sir Charles's already weakened heart.

'Remember it was Stapleton we saw disguised in London? He needed something to give the dog the scent, so he stole Sir Henry's boot. Selden's death, of course, was an attempt upon Sir Henry's life. I arranged our watch over the dinner at Merripit House because we had to catch him red-handed.'

'But how was he going to claim Baskerville Hall?'

'That, my friend, I cannot tell you. The man was never short of ideas. But now, my dear Watson, we have done enough. Let us take an evening stroll.'